MONSTER and Frog

And The

MAGIC SHOW

For Caiden
R.I.

For Clare Mills
R.A.

Consultant: Prue Goodwin,
Lecturer in literacy and children's books,
University of Reading

ORCHARD BOOKS
338 Euston Road, London NW1 3BH
Orchard Books Australia
Hachette Children's Books
Level 17/207 Kent Street, Sydney NSW 2000

First published in Great Britain in 2006
First paperback publication 2007

A CIP catalogue record for this book is available from the British Library

ISBN 1 84121 548 1 (hardback)
ISBN 1 84362 234 3 (paperback)

1 3 5 7 9 10 8 6 4 2

Printed in China

MONSTER AND FROG

And The

MAGIC SHOW

ROSE IMPEY | RUSSELL AYTO

ORCHARD BOOKS

It is Christmas Eve.
Monster is having a party.
Frog has come to help.

The phone rings.

The magician is ill. He cannot come to the party.

Monster does not know what to do.

But Frog says, "Leave it to me.
I could do a magic show with
my eyes closed."

Monster does not like the sound
of that.

"Trust me," says Frog. "This will
be the best magic show ever."

Monster's friends start to arrive.
Frog goes to get ready.

"What a good party,"
says Monster's sister.
"I am looking forward
to the magic show."

But Monster is not so sure.
He wonders why Frog
is taking so long.

Monster soon finds out.
Frog is all dressed up in a cloak
and a tall black hat.
Frog *looks* like a magician.

He says he will begin with
a card trick.

Monster looks worried.
"Relax," whispers Frog. "I am
an expert at card tricks."

Frog tells Monster to take a card
and show it to the audience.
"But do not let me see it."

14

Then Monster puts it back
in the pack and Frog shuffles
the cards.

Frog takes the top card.
He shows it to Monster.

That is not Monster's card!

Frog tries again.

And again.

"Card tricks are not as easy as they look," says Frog.

He drops the cards all over
the floor.
Everyone laughs and claps.
They think it is a good joke.

Frog says he will do a rope
trick next.
Now Monster is really worried.

"Trust me," whispers Frog.
"Rope tricks are my speciality."

Frog folds the rope. He asks
Monster to cut it into four pieces.
"Now," says Frog, "watch me join
the pieces together again."

"Abra-ca-dabra!" says Frog, and he blows on the pieces of rope. But the rope is still in four pieces.

Frog thinks that rope tricks
are a bit tricky, too.
But everyone laughs again.
They think it is another good joke.

For his last trick Frog asks to
borrow Monster's watch.
He says he will make it disappear.

Monster does not like the sound
of *that*.

"This is my best trick of all," says Frog. He puts the watch in his top hat. He taps the hat with his magic wand.

The hat is empty!

The watch has disappeared!

Monster is *very* surprised.

Frog is a little surprised too.

Everyone claps and claps.
They have really enjoyed the
magic show. But now it is time
to go home.

Monster would like his watch back.
But Frog does not seem to be an
expert at bringing watches back.

"Never mind," says Monster.
"At least one of the tricks worked."

"It is almost midnight!" says Frog.
"Shall we open our presents?"

When Monster gives Frog his
present, Frog is very excited.

"How did you know that
I needed to brush up on my
magic?" asks Frog.

"And how did you know that
I needed a new watch?"
asks Monster.

"Good friends always know," says Frog. "And being good friends is *our* speciality."

ROSE IMPEY ♟ RUSSELL AYTO

Enjoy all these adventures with Monster and Frog!

Monster and Frog and the Big Adventure
ISBN 1 84121 536 8
Monster and Frog Get Fit
ISBN 1 84121 542 2
Monster and Frog and the Slippery Wallpaper
ISBN 1 84121 540 6
Monster and Frog Mind the Baby
ISBN 1 84121 544 9
Monster and Frog and the Terrible Toothache
ISBN 1 84121 534 1
Monster and Frog and the All-in-Together Cake
ISBN 1 84121 546 5
Monster and Frog and the Haunted Tent
ISBN 1 84121 538 4
Monster and Frog and the Magic Show
ISBN 1 84121 548 1

All priced at £8.99

Orchard Colour Crunchies are available from all good bookshops, or can be ordered direct from the publisher: Orchard Books, PO BOX 29, Douglas IM99 1BQ
Credit card orders please telephone 01624 836000
or fax 01624 837033 or visit our Internet site: www.wattspub.co.uk
or e-mail: bookshop@enterprise.net for details.

To order please quote title, author and ISBN
and your full name and address.
Cheques and postal orders should be made payable to 'Bookpost plc.'
Postage and packing is FREE within the UK
(overseas customers should add £1.00 per book).

Prices and availability are subject to change.